NIGHTTIME

Too Afraid to Scream

NIGHTTIME®

Too Afraid to Scream

by **Todd Strasser**

illustrated by **Doug Cushman**

Scholastic Inc.

New York   Toronto   London   Auckland
Sydney   Mexico City   New Delhi   Hong Kong

For Conrad and Enzo Scrivener
T.S.

No part of this publication may be reproduced, stored in a retrieval system, or transmitted in any form or by any means, electronic, mechanical, photocopying, recording, or otherwise, without written permission of the publisher. For information regarding permission, write to Scholastic Inc., Attention: Permissions Department, 557 Broadway, New York, NY 10012.

ISBN-13: 978-0-545-12475-1
ISBN-10: 0-545-12475-1

12 11 10 9 8 7 6 5 4 3 2 1   9 10 11 12 13 14/0

Printed in the U.S.A.   40
This edition first printing, October 2009

CONTENTS

The Phantom Text Messager

Callie Jones was bored. She was sitting in math class while Mr. Burton explained ratios. Ratios were dumb. Quietly, Callie reached into her pocket and took out her cell phone. She held it under the desk where Mr. Burton couldn't see it. She thumbed in a message to her best friend, Tanya Sinclair: **where r u?**

A moment later the answer came back: **science**.

Callie replied: **school so boring!**

DON'T TEXT IN CLASS! came the reply. Callie stared at her phone. She couldn't believe Tanya would say that.

"Callie?" Mr. Burton said sternly from the front of the room.

Callie quickly looked up. "Yes, Mr. Burton?"

"Are you paying attention?" the teacher asked.

"Yes, sir." Callie felt her face grow red. She quietly closed the phone and slid it back into her pocket.

As soon as class ended, Callie went out into the hall. Tanya came out of a classroom nearby.

"Why did you tell me not to text in class?" Callie asked her.

"What are you talking about?" Tanya asked.

"That's what you wrote," Callie said.

"Did not," Tanya said.

"Did, too," insisted Callie.

"You're crazy," Tanya said, and walked away.

Callie's next class was Spanish with Ms. Arnold. As Callie entered the room Ms. Arnold handed her a test sheet and said, "I hope you studied your vocabulary."

Callie gasped. She'd forgotten about the test! She stared at the sheet and realized she only knew half the answers. Class began. The kids around her started writing. Callie quietly took out her phone and sent a text to her friend David: **what does caliente mean?**

A moment later an answer came back: **DON'T CHEAT!**

Callie couldn't believe how jerky her friends were acting today. She texted her friend Maggie and asked what *caliente* meant.

I SAID, DON'T CHEAT! came the reply.

Callie couldn't think of anyone else to text so she put away the phone. After class she went out into the hall. Billy Harmon came toward her. Billy was a silly, scrawny boy with big ears. He had lent her his 20Q the week before, but she'd lost it. Every day he asked Callie to bring it to school.

"Hey, Callie, did you remember my Twenty Questions?" he asked.

"Oh, sorry, Billy," Callie said with a fake smile. "Can you believe I forgot it again?"

Billy's shoulders slumped with disappointment. The corners of his mouth turned down. "This is the third day in a row."

"I promise I'll bring it tomorrow," Callie said. "Gotta get to my next class. See you later."

She was walking down the hall when she felt her phone vibrate. Callie flipped it open. The text message said, **DON'T LIE**.

Callie stopped and looked around. She was certain that someone was playing a trick on her. But who? And why?

Callie lived near the school and each day after dismissal she walked home. It was early January and very cold. She wore a heavy coat. A small white cloud came out of her mouth when she exhaled. As she got close to her house, she saw Mrs. Cole, her neighbor, taking bags of groceries out of her car. Mrs. Cole was old and had a bad hip. She limped and winced in pain when she walked. Callie saw that the back of her car was filled with bags of groceries. Mrs. Cole would have to make a lot of trips to get all those groceries inside.

Callie's cell phone vibrated. She checked the text message: **BE HELPFUL**.

Callie didn't know who was sending her these messages, and she didn't care. She had no intention of helping Mrs. Cole. The old woman should have known that if she bought a lot of groceries she'd have to make a lot of trips.

Callie got home and let herself into her house. Her parents didn't get home from work until 6 P.M. Callie watched television for a while. Then she felt hungry and wanted some candy. She went into the kitchen, but there was nothing sweet.

She wondered if she should go to the candy store. It was the dead of winter and already dark out. Callie knew she wasn't allowed to go out after school alone. Especially when it was dark. But she wanted something sweet. If her mother wanted her to stay home after school, then she should have made sure there was candy in the house.

Callie was putting on her coat when her cell phone vibrated. She felt a nervous chill and opened it: **LISTEN TO YOUR PARENTS**.

Callie closed the phone. She didn't know who was sending her these messages. But just because she was getting them didn't mean she had to listen. She finished putting on her coat, gloves, and hat, and went out into the dark.

Callie felt nervous walking down the dark side-walk. She was glad the candy store was nearby. To get to it, she had to cross an intersection at the bottom of a hill. The intersection was always busy and Callie waited.

The light turned green. Callie stepped off the curb. The phone in her pocket vibrated. Callie flipped open the phone. The message read: **STOP!**

Callie stopped. Suddenly a loud horn blared. Callie looked up. A huge truck barreled through the intersection.

The truck roared past and the wind ruffled Callie's coat. The blood drained from her face. She knew that if she had not stopped to read that message, the truck would have run her over.

Suddenly Callie no longer felt hungry. She just felt scared. She turned and started running back toward home.

While she ran, the phone vibrated again. Callie realized that she was still holding it. With trembling hands she opened the phone and read the message: **THIS IS YOUR LAST CHANCE. FROM NOW ON, LISTEN TO WHAT I SAY!**

Black Cat

"That's bad luck, you know," said the boy with curly red hair. His name was Tim Rupert. He was thin and had freckles.

Misha Snyder looked across the sidewalk at him and his friends. She knew he was talking about her black cat, Sylvester. Sylvester was an outdoor cat. He had just crossed Misha's path on her front lawn.

"Not for me," Misha said. It was cold out. When she spoke, white mist rose from her lips.

Tim shrugged and went back to the football game he was playing with his friends. Every day after school they played football on the street in front of Misha's new house. It was November. Misha and her family had been living there for nearly six months. This was the first time Tim had spoken to her.

Misha stood on her front lawn and watched the boys play. Sylvester stopped and watched, too. Almost every day she watched the boys play in the street after school. They never spoke to her or asked her to join in.

The gray clouds overhead grew darker. To Misha it felt like snow was coming. It was too cold to stay outside, so she went back into her house. She was tired of playing by herself or watching TV every day after school. She went upstairs to her father's office.

Mr. Snyder was short and bald and wore glasses with thick brown frames. He spent every day in his office with his computer and telephone and fax machine. He talked to people all over the world about rubber and wrote articles for magazines called *Rubber News* and *World Rubber.*

He also had a large collection of rubber duckies.

Misha went into her father's office. She didn't notice when Sylvester slipped in behind her. Mr. Snyder was typing on his computer. Misha picked up a rubber duckie with black sunglasses and a blue bill. She squeezed it and it squeaked.

Mr. Snyder stopped typing and looked at her. "Hi, hon, what's up?"

"Nothing." Misha shrugged and put the duckie back. Sylvester sat in the corner. He licked his paw and listened.

"Bored?" Mr. Snyder guessed.

Misha nodded. Her father looked out the window. He could see the boys playing in the street. "They still haven't asked you to play with them?"

Misha shook her head. "I wish there were some girls my age on this block." There were girls who lived on the block, but they were either too young or too old.

"I could drive you to a friend's house if you'd like," said Mr. Snyder.

Misha would have liked that. But so far she'd only made one friend at her new school. The girl's name was Sarah. Every day after school Sarah had a piano lesson or a dance class or gymnastics or a tutor. She hardly ever had time to hang out.

Misha spent the rest of the afternoon reading and drawing. At five o'clock her father went into the kitchen to start dinner. Mrs. Snyder got home from work at 5:45 and the family sat down to eat. Sylvester trotted into the kitchen and ate some food from his bowl. Then he hopped up into Misha's lap. He wanted to be petted.

Mrs. Snyder was tall and thin and had short blond hair. "I just heard on the radio that there may be an ice storm tonight."

"I'll get out the flashlights in case the electricity goes off," said Mr. Snyder.

"Good idea," said Mrs. Snyder. She turned to Misha. "How was your day?"

Misha petted Sylvester and shrugged. "That red-haired boy named Tim finally talked to me. He said Sylvester was bad luck."

"That's silly," said Mr. Snyder. "It just so happens

that in Scotland black cats are said to bring good fortune."

Just then, Sylvester sneezed. Misha scratched him behind the ear.

Mr. Snyder added, "In Italy, if a black cat sneezes it means that something good will happen."

Mrs. Snyder smiled. "I guess something good is going to happen." She turned to her daughter. "What do you think that could be?"

It was easy for Misha to think of what would be good. "Finding a friend who wants to play with me."

Sylvester's ears perked up. He hopped off Misha's lap and trotted out of the kitchen. The corners of Mrs. Snyder's mouth turned down. "Oh, honey, I know it's hard. But we haven't been living here that long. It takes time to make new friends."

"That's what you always say," Misha replied. She crossed her arms and pouted. "We've already lived here for six months. It feels like it's going to take *forever*."

Misha's parents shared a concerned look. Then Mrs. Snyder said, "It's hard for your father and me, too. We haven't made any new friends. Everyone we meet is either too busy or has lots of friends already."

That surprised Misha. She'd never thought about her parents wanting to make friends. But why not? They were people, too. Even if they were grown-ups. But knowing that didn't make her feel any better. Maybe they were a family of losers.

The Snyders had just finished dinner when they heard a tinkling sound against the kitchen window. It sounded as if grains of sand were striking the glass.

"What's that?" Misha asked.

"I'll bet it's the ice storm," Mr. Snyder said. He got up and looked outside. "Yep, it's started. Half rain and half ice. I better get the flashlights."

That evening, Misha watched TV. Outside the freezing rain and ice continued to fall. When it was bedtime, her father came into the den. "Before you go up to bed, I want you to see something."

They went into the living room and her father turned off the lights. "Look outside," he said.

Misha looked out the living room window.

Sylvester hopped up onto the windowsill and also looked. The tree branches and electric lines were covered with ice. Everything glittered.

"Isn't it beautiful?" asked Mr. Snyder.

It was pretty, but Misha felt sad. She stared at their neighbors' brightly lit houses. Inside them were kids who had lots of friends.

Misha went upstairs to her room and got into bed. Sylvester followed. Mrs. Snyder came in and sat down on the edge of the bed. "I know you're lonely," she said, stroking Misha's hair. "But you will make more friends. I promise. It just takes time."

Forever, Misha thought sadly.

Mrs. Snyder went to the doorway to turn off the light. Sylvester jumped up on Misha's bed and curled into a ball beside her.

"Good night, honey," Mrs. Snyder said.

"Good night, Mom," said Misha. She fell asleep listening to Sylvester's soft purr and the tinkle of freezing rain and ice against her window.

Crack! A sudden, loud sound from outside woke Misha. She opened her eyes and wondered if she'd been having a bad dream. She could hear her parents muttering in their bedroom. The sound must have awakened them, too.

"Mom? Dad?" she called. "What was it?"

"Nothing, hon," her father called back. "A tree branch snapped. It's the ice. The branches can't hold the weight. Everything's okay. Go back to sleep."

On the bed beside Misha, Sylvester stretched and yawned. Misha closed her eyes.

Crash! There was a huge boom outside. It sounded like a bomb. It was so loud it made Misha jump. She hopped out of bed and raced through the dark into her parents' bedroom. When she got there, they were already getting out of bed.

"What in the world was that?" Mrs. Snyder asked, nervously.

"I'm scared!" Misha gasped.

Mrs. Snyder put her arm around Misha and they all went to the bedroom window. Mr. Snyder raised the blind. Outside, everything was black. The neighbor's houses were dark shapes.

"What happened?" Misha asked.

"A tree must have fallen on the electric lines,"

said Mr. Snyder. "It's hard to tell because it's so dark. All the lights have gone off."

"It's a good thing you got the flashlights," said Mrs. Snyder.

"Yes, I'll . . ." Mr. Snyder began to say something, then stopped and stared across the room.

"What is it?" Misha asked.

"Look." Mr. Snyder pointed at the night table beside the bed. The digital clock read: 1:47.

"There must be a battery in it," said Mrs. Snyder.

Mr. Snyder turned the switch on his night-light. The light went on.

"That's strange," said Mrs. Snyder.

"I guess only the houses across the street lost electricity," said Mr. Snyder. "It must have something to do with the power grid." He stretched and yawned. "Now that I'm up I think I'll have a cup of tea."

"I'll join you," said his wife.

Misha went back to bed. This time Sylvester didn't curl up beside her. The black cat sat in the doorway with his back to the room. It seemed like he was waiting for something. It wasn't long until Misha fell asleep.

Knock! Knock! Misha woke. It was still dark outside. She felt scared. Who would be knocking on their door at this time of night in the middle of a storm?

She heard the front door creak open, and then the sound of voices. Misha got out of bed and went to the top of the stairs. Sylvester sat halfway down the steps. At the bottom of the stairs, Mr. and Mrs. Snyder were letting people into the house. It was the Gilberts, who lived next door. They had a daughter who was two years older than Misha.

"What's going on?" Misha asked.

"The Gilberts lost their heat and electricity," Mrs. Snyder said as she hung their coats in the closet. "They're going to stay with us for the night. Would you mind if their daughter, Samantha, slept on the floor in your room?"

"That's fine," Misha said.

Samantha Gilbert had long brown hair and bright, friendly eyes. She started up the stairs. "Hi." She gave Misha a cheerful smile. "We saw the lights on in your house. You're the only ones on the street with electricity. Isn't that weird?"

"I guess," Misha said.

She was helping Samantha get settled in the bedroom when there was another knock on the front door. Misha went back to the staircase. This time Tim and his family came in wearing winter clothes glistening with rain and ice. They stood by the front closet and spoke to Misha's parents. Sylvester rubbed against Tim's leg. When Tim saw Misha, he waved up at her. "Hi."

Misha waved back. Mrs. Snyder looked up at her daughter. "Can you fit Becky up there?"

Becky was Tim's little sister.

"Sure," said Misha.

Becky went up the stairs, clutching her teddy bear.

But that wasn't the end. Two more families came over. Soon five girls were crowded on the floor of Misha's bedroom. They talked and laughed like it was a sleepover.

Misha was having more fun than she'd had in a long time. But she was worried that if they didn't go to sleep soon they would be too tired for school the next day. But Samantha Gilbert said that with all the ice on the streets there wouldn't be any school.

Finally, around 3 AM, they turned off the lights and fell asleep.

The girls slept almost until noon. When they got up, Mrs. Snyder and Tim's mother, Mrs. Rupert, made everyone a big breakfast. All the kids from the block sat around the table, eating and talking. Tim said that after breakfast they should all get their ice skates. Then they could go skating on the street before the sand trucks came.

The kids had fun skating on the ice-covered street. Then they went around collecting big icicles and made an icicle fort. Soon the power came back on and they all went to Samantha's house, where Mrs. Gilbert made them hot chocolate. By then it was getting dark and everyone was tired.

Back home Misha took off her winter jacket, hat, and gloves. Sylvester rubbed against her leg and purred.

"Did you have fun today?" Mrs. Snyder asked.

"Sure did," Misha said with a big smile. She scratched Sylvester behind the ear.

"So I guess it didn't take forever to make friends," said Mrs. Snyder.

Suddenly, Sylvester sneezed. Misha looked down at the cat and remembered how he'd also sneezed the night before. And how theirs was the only house on the whole street that had electricity during the storm. The black cat stared back at Misha and she thought she saw a glint in his eye. *Maybe it didn't take forever to make friends . . . when you had a good-luck cat.*

The Face in the Flames

The campfire crackled. Orange and yellow flames leapt up from the burning logs. Glowing sparks rose into the dark. Six girls and their camp counselor sat around the fire, roasting marshmallows. The campfire was a weekly event at Camp Pride.

"Do you know what happens if you stare into the flames?" asked the counselor. Her name was Lizanne. She was a tall, thin girl with straight brown hair and thick brown eyebrows.

The girls shook their heads.

"They say you can see the face of the last person you lied to," said Lizanne.

"Really?" gasped a girl named Debra. She had curly dark hair and pink cheeks. Her Camp Pride T-shirt was stretched tight around her chubby tummy. Debra was the sort of girl who believed anything you told her.

"Definitely," said a sharp-tongued girl named Anna. "And if you eat more than five roasted marshmallows in one night, you blow up to the size of a weather balloon."

The other girls around the campfire giggled. Anna was an expert at saying mean things. The other girls were secretly glad that Anna was picking on Debra, because that meant that she was not picking on them.

"That's not true," Debra said. But then she glanced at her counselor, Lizanne, just to make sure. "Is it?"

"I never heard that before," Lizanne said.

Debra felt better. But just to be safe, she ate only five roasted marshmallows that night.

A few days later, Anna decided to start a secret club. She invited three of the girls in the bunk to join. But she told them not to tell Debra, or a girl named Mindy, who was tall and clumsy. It wasn't long before Debra noticed something strange. Nearly every day Anna and the three girls went off by themselves. Debra and Mindy were never invited.

The next day during arts and crafts, Debra said to Anna, "Why do you and the others go off and leave Mindy and me behind?"

Anna pretended not to know what Debra was talking about. "We don't do that."

"It happens almost every day," said Debra.

"We don't do it on purpose," Anna lied.

That night was the weekly campfire. The girls gathered wood and built the fire. Then they roasted marshmallows.

"See any faces?" asked Lizanne.

Anna wondered why the counselor had asked that question. Then she remembered the story about looking at the flames and seeing the face of the last person you lied to. That was silly. Anna slid a marshmallow onto the end of her stick and held it up to the fire.

Then the strangest thing happened. A face slowly appeared in the flames. Anna blinked hard. She was sure it was her imagination. She looked into the flames again. The face looked like Debra's. Anna bit her lip and furrowed her brow. She glanced to her right where Debra sat, roasting a marshmallow. Then she looked back at the fire. Debra's face was still there! How could that be?

"Anna, watch your marshmallow," said Lizanne.

Anna had been so busy looking at the face in the flames that she'd forgotten about her marshmallow. It had caught fire and was burned to a crisp.

Anna put a new marshmallow on her stick. But when she looked at the flames, there was Debra's face again! Anna's heart began to beat hard. She didn't understand how this could be happening. But she couldn't ask if anyone else saw the face. Because then they would know that she'd lied to Debra.

Anna roasted her marshmallow, but she didn't eat it. She'd lost her appetite.

"Is something wrong, Anna?" Lizanne asked.

"No, nothing," Anna said. She spent the rest of the evening trying not to look at the flames. But every time she peeked, Debra's face was still there.

The next day, a girl in the bunk named Caroline had a birthday. At dinner, Lizanne gave Caroline a small birthday cake with ten candles. Anna and the other girls stared at the candle flames. Suddenly Debra's face appeared! Anna's eyes widened in fear. She gasped and felt faint. She wanted to jump up from the table and run away. But she couldn't risk the other girls asking her why. She was very glad when Caroline blew out the candles.

On the way back to the bunk, Anna walked with Lizanne.

"Remember what you said about staring into a fire and seeing a face?" Anna said.

"Yes," said Lizanne.

"I was just wondering," Anna said. "If it was true, how could a person make it stop?"

Lizanne smiled. "I think if she promised that she'd never lie or be mean to anyone ever again, then it would stop."

"That's all?" Anna asked, surprised. It sounded too easy.

"That's all," said Lizanne.

Now it was Anna's turn to smile. That night in bed, she closed her eyes and promised that she would never lie or be mean again.

Five days passed and then came another campfire night. The girls gathered wood and watched while Lizanne lit the fire. Anna was eager to see if what Lizanne had said was true. It still seemed too easy. All she had to do was promise that she'd never lie again, and the face in the fire would disappear.

Flames began to rise from the sticks and branches. The other girls started to roast marshmallows. But Anna just stared.

At first all she saw were the flames.

Then a face began to appear.

Anna gasped.

The face she saw . . . was hers!

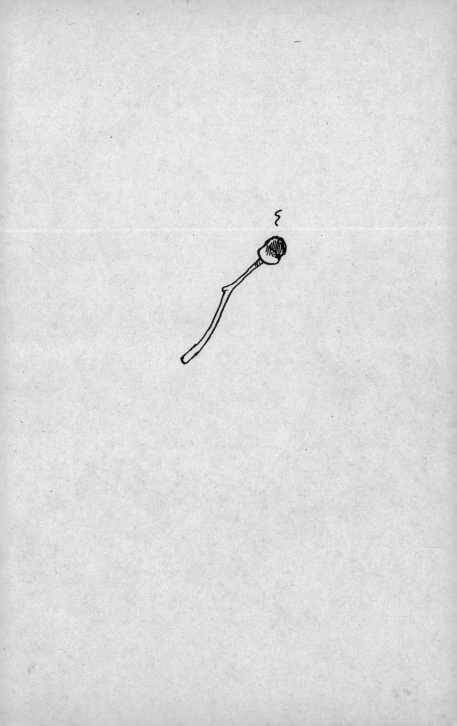

The Skeleton's Foot

"Oh, my gosh!" Holly Davis gasped. "Mom!"

Holly and her family were sifting through the soil and gravel on the side of a small hill. They were wearing rubber boots and raincoats.

Dr. Davis hurried across the rocks and dirt toward her daughter. "What is it?" she asked. Dr. Davis wasn't a medical doctor. She was a professor of archeology. She had taken her family camping after a week of heavy rains and mudslides.

Holly pointed. Sticking out of the ground were small bones.

"Well, I'll be," Dr. Davis said. She bent down and brushed away some dirt with her gloved fingers. Now Holly saw more bones. They were shaped like a hand.

"Arthur!" Dr. Davis shouted. "Come see what Holly found!"

Holly's father scrambled toward them. He was leading Holly's younger sister, Danielle, by the hand.

"What is it?" Mr. Davis asked.

"Holly found part of a skeleton," Dr. Davis said excitedly.

"What kind of skeleton?" Danielle asked nervously.

"I'm certain it must be human," Dr. Davis exclaimed.

"Oh, yuck!" Danielle cried and tried to pull away from her father. "Get me out of here!"

"Hold on," said Mr. Davis. He held Danielle's hand tightly. "You know this is important to your mother."

"Good for her," Danielle said. "But I don't want to see any skeletons. Let me go!"

Holly's younger sister yanked her hand away and scurried down the hill toward the tents.

Mr. Davis let out a frustrated sigh. "Holly, go keep an eye on your sister. I'll stay here and help your mother."

Holly went down the hill. She was secretly glad she wouldn't have to stay and help dig up those bones. The truth was, she didn't like skeletons either.

At the bottom of the hill were two orange tents. One was for Holly's parents and the other was for Holly and Danielle. Between the two tents was a circle of stones for the fire. Holly pulled off her muddy boots and crawled into the tent she shared with her sister. Danielle was inside, sitting with her legs crossed. She was playing with her dolls.

"I hate camping," Danielle muttered. "I hate digging around in dirt. Why can't we go on normal vacations like other kids?"

"Because other kids have normal parents," Holly answered. She wasn't trying to be funny.

"Why can't we have normal parents?" Danielle whined.

Holly couldn't answer that question. Somehow, she and her sister had gotten stuck with an archeologist and an astronomer. Other kids went to Disney World or beach resorts. The Davises went to archeological digs and observatories.

Holly spent the rest of the afternoon reading. Danielle played with her dolls. Around dinner time, Mr. Davis came down the hill and started the fire. Holly crawled out of the tent and looked up the hill. Her mother was still digging.

"Did she find more bones?" Holly asked.

"Looks like a whole skeleton," her father replied as he added sticks to the fire. "The bones are scattered along the face of the hill. Your mom thinks the recent rains washed them down."

Together Holly and her father made dinner. After a while, Danielle came out of the tent. "Can we go home?" she asked.

"Tomorrow morning," said Mr. Davis.

"Why not tonight?" Danielle asked.

"Because," said Mr. Davis.

It was getting dark when Dr. Davis finally came down the hill.

"How's it going?" her husband asked.

"Fantastic," Holly's mother answered. "It looks like almost the entire skeleton. I just wish we'd found him sooner."

"How do you know it's a him?" Holly asked.

"I can tell by the bones," answered her mother. She gazed across the fire at her husband. "Are you sure we have to leave tomorrow? If I could just have one more day..."

"I have to go back," said Mr. Davis. "The kids really want to get home, too. Besides, what difference would one more day make?"

"It would give me the time to find the one thing that's missing," said Dr. Davis.

"What's that?" asked Holly.

"His right foot," said her mother.

"Ugh!" Danielle shivered. "Gross!"

The Davis's sat around the fire and ate dinner. By now it was dark. Dr. Davis stared up at the sky as the moon rose over the hill. "Arthur, is that a full moon?"

Mr. Davis looked. The moon was round and bright. "Yes. And it's not just any full moon. It's a blue moon."

"It's not blue," said Danielle.

"A blue moon isn't blue," her father said. "There's supposed to be one full moon each month. But sometimes there's a second one and it's called a blue moon, and . . ."

Suddenly Mr. Davis stopped speaking, and stared at his wife.

"And what, Dad?" Holly asked.

"Nothing," said Mr. Davis.

"Come on, Dad," Holly said. "What were you going to say?"

Mr. Davis didn't answer. He just stared at his wife.

"Dad?" said Danielle.

"It wasn't important," said Dr. Davis. She covered her mouth with her hand and yawned. "It's been a long day. We should go to sleep."

Holly hated when her parents started to talk about something and then decided the kids shouldn't hear. Then they'd pretend they weren't talking about anything.

But she also knew that there was no point in arguing. Once they'd made up their minds, they wouldn't change.

Soon it was time to go to sleep. The girls went into their tent and crawled into their sleeping bags. Danielle closed her eyes and fell asleep right away. Holly lay on her back and stared up at the ceiling of the tent. The ground under her was bumpy. Even with the foam sleeping mat, she could feel something poking her in the back. Holly knew that to get rid of the pointy thing she would have to leave the tent. She didn't want to do that.

In the moonlight, the shadows of the tree branches made patterns on the tent's fabric. Holly turned on her side so the pointy thing wouldn't poke her. After a while she closed her eyes and fell asleep.

In the middle of the night, a sound woke her.

Holly opened her eyes. She wondered if some animal had made the sound. She wasn't scared, because her mother had said there were no dangerous animals around. Only deer and raccoons and squirrels.

Holly closed her eyes. But then she heard the sound again. This time it was closer. Holly knew it wasn't an animal sound. It was more like a dull rattle.

Holly rolled onto her back in her sleeping bag. She could feel the pointy thing poking her as she stared up at the shadows against the tent. Soon she heard the rattling sound again. A little bit closer and a little bit louder.

Holly's heart began to beat faster. Now she could hear other sounds. Not just the rattle, but a scrape as if something was being dragged along the ground.

And it was coming even closer.

Holly's breaths became shallow and quick. She wanted to yell, but she didn't want to scare Danielle. What if it was only some harmless animal?

The rattling and scraping sounds came closer and grew louder. Holly's heart banged in her chest. She was breathing so fast she feared she might faint. Didn't anyone else hear it?

Holly was trembling all over. What could be out there?

Suddenly a shadow appeared against her tent. Holly caught her breath. *Oh, no! It couldn't be!* Inside the tent, Holly clenched her fists and stifled the urge to scream.

The shadow went around the tent twice. Holly had never been so scared in her entire life.

Then the shadow began to move away. Holly lay in her sleeping bag, shivering with fear. The rattling and scraping sounds grew fainter and fainter.

For a long time Holly lay on her back, staring at the ceiling of the tent. Once again she could feel the pointy thing poking her in the back. Holly knew there was no way she would leave the tent now. Finally, she rolled onto her side and fell asleep.

"Holly?" Someone was shaking her shoulder.

Holly opened her eyes and looked up into her father's face.

"Time to get up," Mr. Davis said.

Holly yawned. She felt very tired. "Can't I sleep a little longer?"

"No, we have to pack up and leave," said her father. "This isn't like you. Usually you're the first one up. Now, come on, get dressed."

Holly felt very tired. She slowly got dressed and crawled out of the tent. Danielle and her father were taking down the other tent.

"Where's Mom?" Holly asked with a yawn.

"She went to take one last look," said Mr. Davis.

Holly looked up the hill. Her mother stood with one hand on her hip. With the other hand she scratched her head. Finally she came back down.

"That's the darnedest thing I've ever seen," she said.

"What are you talking about?" Danielle asked.

"Uh, nothing," said her father.

"Not this again," Holly complained. "Tell us."

Her parents shared a look.

"The blue moon is over," said Mr. Davis to Dr. Davis.

"That's true," said Dr. Davis. She turned to Holly. "There's an old saying that on a blue moon, skeletons come out of their graves. They gather their bones and walk the earth."

Holly caught her breath.

"I used to think it was just a crazy old story," her mother went on. She pointed at the hill. "But the skeleton that was there yesterday is gone. I just don't understand how it could go anywhere without one foot."

Holly's heart began to beat hard. She looked back at her tent and stared at the ground around it.

"What are you looking at?" Mr. Davis asked.

Holly pointed a trembling finger at the ground.

Mr. Davis kneeled down and looked. Dr. Davis and Danielle joined him.

"What is it?" asked Danielle.

"It's a track," said Mr. Davis. "It looks like a skeleton's left foot and some sort of pole."

"As if it was using a crutch," said Holly's mother.

"And it went around the tent twice," said Mr. Davis. "As if it were searching for something. But what?"

Holly knew the answer. She'd lain on it all night long.

Track 13

Talya Burlingham and her mother, Mrs. Valerie DeChamp Burlingham, had decided to take the overnight train to Florida. Other people flew, but Talya and her mother found that airports were too crowded and noisy. And airplanes were so cramped. The Burlinghams liked to spread out: They believed that they deserved to travel in comfort.

Besides, they would never, ever, think of putting

Fru in a cage. Fru was their teacup terrier. The thought of Fru being kept with the luggage was horrible.

Talya and her mother took a cab to Hanover Station. The cabdriver was very rude. He refused to take the route Mrs. Burlingham told him to take. He also drove much too fast. And he *dropped* their luggage on the curb outside the railroad station.

"What a horrible man," Mrs. Burlingham huffed while they waited on the sidewalk for a porter to come get their luggage.

"I agree," said Talya. "I hope you didn't tip him."

"Certainly not," said her mother. "He didn't deserve a penny."

They waited and waited for the porter. When no porter came, Mrs. Burlingham sighed loudly. "You simply cannot get good service these days. Wait here with Fru while I go find someone."

Talya waited. Soon her mother returned with a porter. "Be careful," she told the man. "This is very expensive luggage."

The porter put the luggage on his cart and wheeled it into the station. Talya and Mrs. Burlingham followed. Talya carried Fru. She did not want the little dog to dirty its paws on the ground.

Mother and daughter went to the ticket window. Inside was a young woman with black hair.

"I am Valerie DeChamp Burlingham and I have reserved two tickets for the overnight train to Florida," Talya's mother announced.

The young woman checked her computer. "I'm sorry, but I'm not showing that reservation."

"That's ridiculous," Mrs. Burlingham huffed. "I made the reservation myself."

"I'm sorry, ma'am, but it's not here," said the young woman in the ticket booth.

"Mother, ask to speak to the manager," Talya suggested. Like her mother, Talya hated being treated rudely.

Mrs. Burlingham asked to see the manager. When he arrived, she insisted that she had made the reservation. She added that the dark-haired young woman had been extremely rude. The manager said he was sorry, but said that nothing could be done.

Mrs. Burlingham argued that she deserved much better treatment than this. She asked to speak to the manager's boss. In the meantime, Talya noticed an old man standing at the end of the long row of ticket windows. He wore a ticket taker's uniform, and waved quietly at Talya.

Talya walked toward him. When she got close, the old man whispered, "I can help you and your mother. That manager doesn't understand that you are important and cultured people. You deserve better."

This was music to Talya's ears. The old man went into the last ticket booth. He pulled open an old wooden drawer. "Ah ha!" he said. "It's just as I suspected. Here are your tickets." He handed Talya a white envelope. "Your train is on track thirteen. You'd better hurry. It's going to leave soon."

Clutching the envelope, Talya rushed back to

her mother. Mrs. Burlingham was still complaining. She said that if they didn't find her reservation, she would sue the railroad company.

Talya whispered in her mother's ear that she had the tickets. Then she and her mother and the porter hurried toward track 13.

They barely made it. The porter put the last piece of luggage on the luggage rack in their cabin. The train began to move. The porter hopped off. Mrs. Burlingham didn't tip him because he'd banged a suitcase against one of the train's steps.

The train began to pick up speed. Talya and her mother settled into their cabin. They smiled at each other. Mrs. Burlingham took Fru out of the traveling case and placed the little dog on her lap.

"You see, Talya," Mrs. Burlingham said. "Things always work out. We always get what we deserve."

Suddenly, the train car lurched to the left. One of the suitcases fell out of the luggage rack. It crashed to the floor and burst open. Clothes spilled out. With a yelp, Fru tumbled out of Mrs. Burlingham's lap.

Slam! The train car lurched to the right. Another suitcase fell and burst open. The floor around the Burlinghams' feet was covered with clothes.

Wham! The train swung to the left. Talya cried out. She felt like she was on a roller coaster.

The train slammed back and forth. Talya and her mother held the armrests as tight as they could. Soon all their expensive luggage had crashed to the floor and broken open.

"This is horrible!" Mrs. Burlingham cried. "I must speak to the conductor."

Talya's mother went out into the aisle to look for the conductor. Talya stayed in the cabin. She held Fru with one arm. With her other hand she held the armrest. The train shook so hard that she felt sick.

Mrs. Burlingham was gone for a long time. Finally she came back to the cabin. She looked pale and frightened. Her hair had come loose and her clothes were twisted and wrinkled. She sat down and held on tight while the train continued its sickening ride.

"Did you find the conductor?" Talya asked.

Mrs. Burlingham shook her head. Her eyes were wide with fear. "There is no conductor."

Talya didn't understand. "What about the other passengers?"

"There are no other passengers," her mother answered.

The train shook and bucked like a wild bull. Talya still didn't understand. "How can that be?"

"I don't know," Mrs. Burlingham said.

All night long the train slammed back and forth. Mother and daughter held on. Their beautiful clothes lay in a heap on the floor. Their expensive luggage was broken. They never got a second of sleep. It was the most miserable trip of their lives.

I don't deserve this! Talya thought over and over.

Morning came. Outside the day began to brighten. The train stopped shaking and slowed down. Talya and her mother were exhausted from the long, violent ride. They packed their clothes back into the broken suitcases and tied the luggage closed with belts and scarves.

Finally, the train stopped. Wearily, Talya and her mother dragged their suitcases off. They were both bruised and exhausted. *At least we're in Florida*, Talya thought.

But something was wrong. The air didn't feel warm and moist. It felt cool and dry. Talya looked around. They were in Hanover Station!

Mrs. Burlingham must have realized the same thing. Stunned and confused, they stood on the train platform. Suddenly, Talya pointed. "It's him!"

Coming toward them was the old man who'd given them the tickets the night before. Filled with anger, Talya hurried toward him.

"Those tickets you gave us didn't take us to Florida," she said. "Instead they took us on the worst train trip ever. And now we're right back where we started."

"It certainly was not what we asked for," Mrs. Burlingham huffed.

"No, it wasn't," said the old man. "But it certainly was what you deserved."

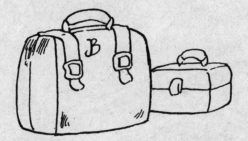

The Hitchhikers

The Stoppard family was driving through the dark to Crystal Lake. They'd just had a big dinner at a diner beside the road.

"Do you have to go so fast?" asked Mrs. Stoppard while her husband drove along a road called North Forest.

"Sam Roberts said he'd wait for us," Mr. Stoppard replied. "We're already behind schedule. I don't want to keep him waiting."

"Why doesn't he leave the cabin door open for us?" asked Mrs. Stoppard. "That's what he did last year."

Mr. Stoppard knew why, but he didn't want to tell his wife. Not while their daughter, Lacey, was in the car. Lacey was in the backseat, reading with a flashlight. Lacey loved to read. She'd brought half a dozen books for the weekend.

"I'll tell you later," said Mr. Stoppard. Then he tilted his head toward the backseat. Mrs. Stoppard understood.

"I love going up to the lake during the off-season," Mrs. Stoppard said. "There's no one around. It's so peaceful and quiet. And we always get cabin three, the one with the best view."

"Sam said we'll be the only ones staying at the cabins this weekend," said Mr. Stoppard.

In the backseat, Lacey Stoppard continued reading with the flashlight.

A little while later raindrops began to splat against the windshield. Mr. Stoppard switched on the wipers. "I think they said there would be some rainstorms tonight," he said. "But by tomorrow it'll be nice again."

The rain came down harder. Lacey could hear it drumming against the roof of the car. Mr. Stoppard slowed the car.

Suddenly Lacey heard a sharp intake of breath. It had come from her mother. Lacey looked up from her book. A woman and a small boy were standing beside the road in the rain.

"Bruce, you have to stop," Mrs. Stoppard told her husband.

Mr. Stoppard slowed down, but didn't stop.

"Bruce?" Mrs. Stoppard said questioningly.

"It could be a trick," Mr. Stoppard said.

"You have to stop," Lacey's mother insisted. "They were all alone in the rain."

Mr. Stoppard pulled the car to the side of the road. By now they were more than a quarter mile past the woman and child. Lacey looked out the back window. The woman and boy were hurrying toward the car.

"I don't like it," Mr. Stoppard said. "What are they doing out here in the middle of nowhere?"

"Maybe their car broke down," Mrs. Stoppard said.

"I didn't see a car," said Mr. Stoppard. "Did you?"

"Now that you mention it, I didn't," Mrs. Stoppard admitted.

Lacey was still watching out the back window. The woman and boy were getting closer.

"So, I repeat," Mr. Stoppard said. "What were they doing there?"

"I'm sure there's a good answer," said Mrs. Stoppard. "We can't just leave them."

"Let someone else pick them up," Mr. Stoppard said.

"Who?" Mrs. Stoppard asked. "It's been a long time since we saw another car."

The woman and child were getting closer. Lacey could almost see their faces.

"Listen," Mr. Stoppard said, "if it was just you and me, I wouldn't care. But we've got Lacey, too. What if they are up to no good?"

Mrs. Stoppard looked over the seat at her daughter. She pressed her lips together as if trying to decide what to do. By now, Lacey could see the rain-soaked faces of the woman and boy. Their wet hair was plastered to their heads.

Mr. Stoppard seemed to make up his mind about something. "I'll tell you why Sam Roberts didn't leave the cabin door open for us. They've been having some problems up here lately. People have been breaking in and stealing. That sort of thing."

Mrs. Stoppard stared at her husband, and then at her daughter. "All right, for Lacey's sake," she said.

Mr. Stoppard pressed on the gas and steered the car back onto the road. Through the rear window, Lacey saw the woman and boy stop running. The boy's mouth fell open with surprise as the car pulled away from them. The woman's face filled with disappointment.

Lacey watched in the rearview mirror until the woman and child disappeared into the dark. When she turned around, her mother was looking at her. "Do you understand why we didn't pick them up?"

Lacey nodded. "They might have been bad people. They might have hurt us."

"They're probably not bad people," her mother said. "But there's no way to know for certain. We didn't want to take a chance with you in the car."

Lacey nodded and started to read again. A little while later she heard a strange sound, like teeth chattering. She looked up. The car felt warm. Her parents were staring straight ahead into the night.

"Did you hear that?" Lacey asked.

"Hear what?" asked Mrs. Stoppard.

"That sound. Like chattering teeth."

"It must have been the road," said Mr. Stoppard.

Lacey started reading again. But a moment later, she heard another sound. It sounded like someone's stomach growling hungrily. Lacey looked up. Neither of her parents seemed to notice. They'd all just had a big dinner. There was no reason for anyone's stomach to growl.

Lacey looked back at her book. But now she heard a whimper and a soft shush. It sounded like a mother trying to calm an upset child.

"Mom, Dad, I keep hearing things," Lacey said nervously.

Mrs. Stoppard looked over the seat at her. "Like what?"

"Like a woman and a child," Lacey said. "Like the ones we left in the rain."

In the front seat, Mr. and Mrs. Stoppard shared a look. "That's not possible," her father said.

"But I heard them," Lacey insisted. "I'm sure I did. I'm scared. Can I sit up front with you?"

"Yes, of course," Mrs. Stoppard said.

Mr. Stoppard stopped the car. The rain had slowed to a drizzle. Lacey got into the front and sat between her mother and father. Mr. Stoppard started to drive again. Lacey didn't hear any more sounds. Soon she fell asleep.

Later that night, the Stoppards arrived at the cottages by the lake. The lights were on in cabin #3. Inside, they could see Sam Roberts waiting for them.

The Stoppards carried their bags inside. Sam held the door for them. He was a tall man with dark hair and a thick mustache.

"I'm sorry we're late," Mr. Stoppard said. "We were slowed down by the rain."

"And the hitchhikers," added Lacey.

Sam frowned. "Hitchhikers?"

"A woman and a boy," said Mrs. Stoppard. "In the rain. We almost stopped for them, but then Bruce told us about the trouble you've been having around here. We got scared, for Lacey's sake."

"A woman and a boy," Sam repeated. "That's so strange."

"Why?" asked Mr. Stoppard.

"Because I've heard about them before," said Sam. "Other people have reported seeing them. But only in bad weather." He went to a bookshelf and pulled out an old scrapbook. Inside were yellow newspaper clippings. Sam turned the pages and then pressed his finger down on an old story.

Lacey gasped when she saw the photograph. "It's them!"

Mrs. Stoppard read the headline out loud. "'Mother and son disappear in winter storm. Last seen hitchhiking on North Forest Road.'"

"That's where we saw them!" Mr. Stoppard said.

"Look at the date," said Sam.

"Nineteen fifty-five!" said Mrs. Stoppard. "That boy would be almost sixty now."

"And his mother would be an old woman," said Lacey.

Sam nodded. "All I can say is you're not alone. Plenty of other people have reported seeing them. Some have even said they felt like they were riding in a car with them."

"That's how I felt!" Lacey cried and threw her arms around her mother.

"Don't be scared," Sam said. "No one has ever reported seeing those two anywhere but on North Forest Road. So you don't have to worry. You can take another route home and never go on that road again."

It was late and Sam had to leave. Mr. Stoppard locked the cabin door. Lacey looked again at the story in the scrapbook.

"Are you sure it's them?" Mr. Stoppard asked.

"I'm positive," said Lacey.

"I agree," said Mrs. Stoppard. "There's no mistaking them."

"I'm scared," Lacey said. She was still trembling and holding her mother's hand.

"Now, now, there's nothing to be afraid of," said Mrs. Stoppard. "You heard Sam. They've only been seen on North Forest Road. We'll take a different road home."

"You promise?" Lacey asked.

"You bet," said Mr. Stoppard. "I don't want to see those ghosts again either."

They put Lacey to bed and stayed with her until she fell asleep.

The next morning Mr. Stoppard woke up before his wife and daughter. He went into the kitchen and made himself scrambled eggs and toast for breakfast. He sat by the window and ate. The small resort was empty. Theirs was the only cabin with a car in front of it.

Mr. Stoppard thought about what had happened the night before. He'd never believed in ghosts, but last night proved that he was wrong. The good news was that as long as he stayed away from North Forest Road, he'd never have to see those ghosts again.

Suddenly the fork fell out of his hand. It clattered to the table. Mr. Stoppard sat with his mouth open and a stunned look on his face.

Across the yard, a woman was holding the door to cabin #1 open. A boy was going out to play. There was no car parked in front of the cabin.

It was them.

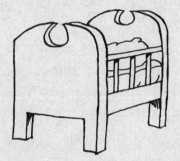

Hush, Little Babies

Sophie Palmer's mother was expecting twins. Sophie was eight and she had a brother, Alan, who was five. She also had a little sister named Brittney who was two.

"I guess we're going to have to move to a bigger house," Mr. Palmer said one night at dinner. "This house only has two bedrooms. We're in one and Sophie, Alan, and Brittney are in the other. We don't have room for two more kids."

"But we can't afford a three-bedroom house," said Mrs. Palmer.

"I'll look around," said Mr. Palmer. "Maybe we can find a bargain."

Each week Mrs. Palmer got bigger as the twins grew. Finally one night at dinner she said, "These babies are due in three months. If we don't find a new home soon, I'll have to have them here."

Mr. Palmer nodded gravely. "There is one three-bedroom house we can afford."

"Why haven't you told me about it?" asked Mrs. Palmer.

Mr. Palmer took a deep breath and let it out reluctantly. "I'll tell you after dinner."

Sophie knew what that meant. It was something Mr. Palmer didn't want the children to hear.

After dinner, Mrs. Palmer put Brittney to bed. Mr. Palmer read to Alan. After a while Brittney and Alan fell asleep. Sophie's parents went into the kitchen to talk. They didn't know that Sophie was standing outside the kitchen door, listening.

"Taking care of three young kids is hard," Mrs.

Palmer complained. "I don't know how we're going to manage with five."

"We'll find a way," said Mr. Palmer.

"So tell me about the house you found," said Mrs. Palmer.

"It's a nice house and I think you'd like it," said Mr. Palmer. "The problem is that something bad happened there."

"What happened?" asked Mrs. Palmer.

"The people who lived there had a son about Sophie's age," Mr. Palmer said. Then he dropped his voice and said something Sophie couldn't hear.

A few weeks later at dinner one night, both of Sophie's parents were smiling. "Guess what?" Mr. Palmer said. "Today your mom and I bought a bigger house. We'll move in next month."

Sophie gasped. It had to be the house where something bad happened to that boy!

A month passed and then the family moved. Sophie liked the new house. The room she shared with Alan and Brittney was larger than their old bedroom. And there was a bigger backyard to play in. Sophie helped her mother prepare the nursery for the twins. The only thing that bothered Sophie was the faint smell of smoke that lingered in the corners.

When the twins were born they were ruddy-faced and squawked like little birds. Now Mrs. Palmer had five children to take care of. At least once a night the twins woke up and cried until they were fed. And sometimes Brittney woke in the middle of the night and wanted a cookie. Once in a while Alan woke up because he'd had a nightmare. When that happened Mrs. Palmer would have to sit with him until he fell back to sleep.

Sophie's mother was tired and irritable all the time. She often snapped at Alan and Brittney, and she constantly made Sophie do chores. Sometimes at night Sophie would wake up when the twins began crying. She would hear her parents in their bedroom arguing about who should get up and go to them.

"It's your turn," Mrs. Palmer would groan.

"I have to go to work early tomorrow," Mr. Palmer complained.

"So do I," said Mrs. Palmer. "Taking care of five kids is hard work, too. Especially the twins. As soon as I get one to stop crying, the other starts."

"The doctor said we should stop getting up when they cry," said Mr. Palmer. "He said that's how they learn to sleep through the night."

The next night the twins cried for a long time. Sophie lay in bed and listened while her parents argued over who should feed them. After a while, the babies stopped crying.

"What happened?" Sophie heard her mother ask her father.

"I guess they got tired and went back to sleep," said Mr. Palmer. "That's what the doctor said would happen."

The next night the same thing happened. The babies started to cry and Mr. and Mrs. Palmer started to argue. Then the babies stopped crying, and Sophie's parents went back to sleep.

The next night when the babies cried, Mr. and Mrs. Palmer didn't argue. They just waited until the crying stopped.

"It's just like the doctor predicted," Mr. Palmer said with a yawn.

By now summer had arrived and the days were long and hot. One day Sophie stayed outside all day running and playing with her friends. That night when the babies started crying, Sophie woke up feeling thirsty. She decided to go to the bathroom and drink some water. Sophie got out of bed and walked down the hall to the bathroom. She passed the nursery. The babies had stopped crying. The door was open.

Sophie froze and stared.

Inside the nursery was a boy about her age. Sophie knew he wasn't real because she could almost see through him. But he was real enough to be able to hold one twin in each arm. He was rocking them gently.

Sophie wanted to scream, but she was afraid the boy would drop the babies. Instead, she just stared.

The boy stared back at her. Sophie could see that it wasn't easy for him to hold one baby in each arm. He gently put the sleeping babies back in their cribs.

Then, before Sophie's astonished eyes, he slowly disappeared.

The next day Mr. Palmer was washing the car. Sophie went outside and watched him for a little while. Then she said, "Dad, I heard that something bad happened in this house. Would you tell me? I think I'm old enough to know."

Mr. Palmer gazed at her as if trying to make up his mind. Then he nodded. "All right, if you really want to know. The real estate agent told me that the family who lived here before us had a son about your age. He was an only child and he loved taking care of animals. One day his parents got him a puppy. He loved that puppy more than anything. If the puppy barked or cried at night, he would get out of bed and take care of him. Then one night there was a fire. It wasn't a bad fire, but there was a lot of smoke. Everyone got out of the house, but then they heard the puppy bark. Before anyone could stop him, the boy ran back into the house. But before he could find the puppy, he was overcome by smoke."

Sophie nodded. Now she understood.

That night, when the twins started crying,

Sophie quietly got out of bed and hurried into the nursery. The boy was already lifting one of the twins out of its crib. Sophie held her arms out. She and the boy locked eyes. Then the boy handed her the baby. He reached for the other one. Together he and Sophie rocked the babies until they fell asleep.